MW01592941

"It's somewhere between 'Ulysses' and 'iPad for Dummies'. Closer to the latter though."

—herbalt, *amazon reviewer*

"Anyhoodle, [this book is] frigging hilarious... From the copyright pirate warning, to the chapter headings, to line after line of really funny prose, this short is full of whip-sharp dialogue and clever turns of phrase."

—Acesfull, *amazon reviewer*

PRAISE FOR *LACEY NOONAN*

"Noonan's back catalogue covers a great deal of ground, and pretty much humps the shit out of it."

—David Roth, *VICE*

"I adore Lacey Noonan's writing style."

—Leonard Delaney, *author of Conquered by Clippy*

"Lacey Noonan has truly catapulted herself, however knowingly, into the pantheons of greatest American authors (F. Scott Fitzgerald, Mark Twain, etc.), greatest female American authors (Willa Cather, Toni Morrison, etc.), and greatest humans (Jesus, Julius Caesar, etc.) to have ever set foot on this great Earth we call home."

—Brenden, *amazon reviewer*

"...one of the literary masters of our time..."

—Jonathan C. Pike, *amazon reviewer*

P<small>RAISE</small> <small>FOR</small> *A G<small>RONKING TO</small> R<small>EMEMBER</small>*

"We were made aware this weekend that Gronk erotica exists and is being sold on Amazon. Due journalism diligence insisted we purchase this Gronk erotica, give you a full review, and then turn it into an animated movie."
     —*Deadspin*

"'Lacey Noonan,' an author—nay, an American hero—recently penned one of the greatest works of fan fiction we here at Complex Sports had ever seen... We're talking highbrow shit here."
     —*Complex*

"It's been a slow year for people who have been looking for NFL-related erotica novels, but the drought is finally over thanks to author Lacey Noonan (Not pictured above)."
     —*CBSSports.com*

"Rob Gronkowski might just be the hero that the world of erotica needs right now."
     —*Inquisitr.com*

"Rob Gronkowski Erotica Is Here and It's... Something."
     —*Boston.com*

"The western canon is scattered with watershed works of literature penned by American authors...add A Gronking to Remember to that list."
     —Brenden, *amazon reviewer*

"I don't want to live in a world where this book doesn't exist."
     —David B. Hansen, *amazon reviewer*

"Thought this was going to be about the hash browns at Dunkin' Donuts. Disappointing!"
     —happykins, *amazon reviewer*

a

The Dishes Are Done Man!

book

Books by *Lacey Noonan*

Novellas

A Gronking to Remember

A Gronking to Remember 2: Chad Goes Deep in the Neutral Zone

Seduced by the Dad Bod: Book One of the Chill Dad Summer Heat Series

Hot Boxed: How I Found Love on Amazon

The Babysitter Only Rings Once

I Don't Care If My Best Friend's Mom is a Sasquatch, She's Hot and I'm Taking a Shower With Her …Because It's the New Millennium

I Don't Care if My Sasquatch Lover Says the World is Exploding, She's Hot But I Play Bass and There's Nothing Hotter Right Now Than Rap Rock …Because It's the New Millennium • Book 2

Eat Fresh: Flo, Jan and Wendy and the Five Dollar Footlong

Novels

Shipwrecked on the Island of the She-Gods: A South Pacific Trans Sex Adventure

Collections

The Hotness: Five Burning Hot Novellas

A
Cruzmas
Carol

Ted Cruz Takes a Dickens of a Constitutional

Book One in the
• White House Sweet '16 Series •

Lacey Noonan

• *Illustrations by the British Library* •

ISBN: 152275573X
ISBN-13: 978-1522755739

CONTENTS

Special Thanks   i

Chapter 1 ... *The Lonely Oyster*   3

Chapter 2 ... *Fat Magic*   20

Chapter 3 ... *Snowbird*   29

Chapter 4 ... *Prognosticating*   38

Chapter 5 ... *Chubb Rock*   45

Chapter 6 ... *Yuppers*   59

Chapter 7 ... *Flutter and Fade*   77

About the Author   86

More Books by Lacey Noonan   88

A Special, Wonderful Thanks

*Salami, Scary Karl, Ray Cho, J.J. Finestone IV,
Slackervoy, Scotty in 3D, Big Rock,
Jennifer Pusch, Hi Dave*

To *Ricardo Mantalbán*

A Cruzmas Carol

"The passionate pursuer has all the earmarks of a fugitive."
      —Eric Hoffer

"I'm too sexy for my shirt, too sexy for my shirt, so sexy it hurts."
      —Right Said Fred

CHAPTER 1
The Lonely Oyster

Feeling fresher and looking cooler than a head of iceberg lettuce on the first day of harvest, Senator Ted Cruz walked into the back room of the exclusive D.C. establishment Fizzywhigs, scanning the room for pussy.

It was his retirement party after all, and if any man in the joint deserved to get his dick wetter than Neptune's, that man was Ted Cruz.

He had Roberta book the place when he'd decided he wanted out of Washington politics—grown tired of the partisan gridlock, the attention whores and the attention pimps and the attention johns, the pernicious and wasteful government that would never in a million years turn back the downhill slide inaugurated immediately after the Declaration of Independence in 1776.

"What's up, y'all!" he twanged into the crowd, using the honeydew Texas drawl he'd picked up at Princeton while studying for his Bachelor of Arts in Public Policy. Across the room Roberta caught his eye. She was the staffer he'd been crushing on for years. She sipped from a large cocktail glass and looked at him meaningfully with her tender gaze. She touched the side of her nose.

The man of the hour.

Was it on?

This shindig was going to be his big send off. Eight years as a U.S. Senator after all—*pretty dang good*. Experience enough on the Hill to snatch up a high-paying K Street consult gig. From now on he would be a tank driver at a think tank, just like that dreamboat-for-freedom Brad Pitt in the movie *Fury*.

But not much thinking, Ted knew, went into *these* think tanks. Just shoot off some watery whatever-the-hell policy paper every once and while, cribbed from Ayn Rand or Henry Kissinger's Wikipedia pages, and the invisible hands of power would stuff seven figures into the stylish Brooks Brothers pants pockets that bulged now on either side of his immense and thickening manhood.

The assembled crowd turned and saw the man of the hour. Cheers filled the normally-distinguished back room.

Ted smiled and waved, walked into the crowd, shook hands. It was a place where the virtuous and powerful had quietly decided the fates of millions. Well... tonight it was going to be a Redbull-and-Vodka-fueled bone zone, Ted thought, where the fates of hundreds of orgasms hung in the balance.

Hung.

The party began in earnest. Glasses clinked. Hors d'oeuvres levitated high above heads on white gloved hands. An hour or so later, Ted had finagled his way through the piles of DC trash to Roberta. They sat at a table in the corner, faces inches apart, whispering boozily to one another, thick as thieves.

"I can't believe you're leaving me," Roberta said.

Ted looked at her and saw her eyes moistening with tears. Roberta's presence always got

Ted's pilot light flickering. She was a raven-haired, pale skinned beauty from Yale Law. Wide hips like a fertility goddess, snugging the edges of her pantsuit. Gypsy eyes, that mesmerized all who would dare to

A meaningful, tender gaze.

stare. Lovely pink lips that just said, *Good evening, sir. Fancy a wet smooch?*

"Oh, you know I'd never leave you, Bob,"

said Ted.

"But you *are*."

"No I'm not! I'll be right down on K Street. I'll be closer than close. We can have hors d'oeuvres any time." He looked at their table. Ted had watched her down a giant plate of oysters by herself, Virginia bluepoints, and only one bivalve remained. One lonely oyster.

"But it's not just *me* you're leaving," Roberta said, her bosoms heaving. "You're leaving your constituents. Your fellow Americans. They need you!"

"Bah!" Ted interjected.

"*We* need you, Ted," she said and lay her hand on his.

Her hand on his... she might as well have shot lightning from her nipples through her pantsuit and electrocuted him to death with sexual electricity—the feeling was that notable.

"Bah?" Ted interrogated.

"Is there... *anything* I can *do*... to... *persuade* you to stay in the public sector?" she cooed like a lioness.

The hairs on the back of Ted's neck stood on end. A chill thrilled his spine. In his lap his President Johnson hardened with utmost urgency, as

A notable feeling.

did President Johnson after the Gulf of Tonkin incident, and it pressed against the underside of the table. That's how big he was. Big as a Texas bull. The table lifted from the floor ever so slightly and wobbled as if they were at a séance.

Visions of sugarplums danced in Ted's head. He peered through the dusky light of Fizzywhigs' back room at Roberta across the table. *Good old Roberta,* he thought. *Wow. Just look at those tits. Big. Nice big boobies. Great Chief of Staff. I bet she has a wonderful vagina. Just wonderful. Warm, inviting. American. Cherry. Like Martha Washington. Like a colonial bonnet for a dick. Wow. Just wrap it up snug like a weary traveler in a good, honest American home, guarded against unlawful entry or the quartering of occupying armies by the Constitution of the United States. And yet... How wonderful it would be to quarter my soldiers in thine thatched hut, Yankee wench, 'gainst thine wishes. Wow.*

But Ted knew cooler heads must prevail. He saw the downward spiral of government. "No, look, sorry. I can't do it," Ted said finally. The future was calling and it wasn't the public sector. "I have to leave. I never really cared about politics. It's all just a bunch of... hooey."

'Gainst thine wishes. Wow.

Roberta stifled a sob. Tears began to flow from her beautiful eyes, as wet and wide and full of life's mystery as the Reflecting Pool itself.

"Bob…" Ted said.

Roberta began to really wail now. She sobbed heartily, full-bodied. Her tits went up and down like hydraulic pumps. And while this was surely something visually stunning to witness, Ted feared making a scene. He leapt up from his side of the table and sat down next to her on her chair. Each had a cheek on the seat, and their hips touched.

"Roberta… I had no idea you felt this way."

"Please. We need you. I need you. Timmy needs you," she choked through the tears.

"Timmy? Who's—"

"Yeah."

Ted was feeling really hot now. Something in his gut warbled. Was that his heart—his stone dead heart coming to life? He felt the closeness of her body, the warmth of her feminine charms. Of these he wished to partake. He took up her hands in his, so soft (hers). "Look. What did you have in mind?"

"You stay Senator of Texas. Run again. Run *forever*. We all keep our jobs. American government stays small and out of peoples' lives."

"No—not that. I mean, that *would* be great—indivisible, with liberty, under God—but before… About, um, *persuading* me?"

Roberta lifted her face up and turned toward Ted. Their eyes met. Ted gazed into her wet orbs. She was a rare beauty, this Roberta, this Buffalo Nickel of a dime. She spread her lips and smiled, revealing shapely white teeth. Ted smiled back as best he could.

"Hmm, well… let me see, *Senator*," Roberta whispered. He watched her eyes play over his face and witnessed the titillation and flirtation that registered as she alighted on each aspect of his visage: the handsome, pointed nose, the well-proportioned mouth that spoke truth and economic justice, the taut, angular chin, the non-calculating pupils of his eyeballs in the head that contained the brain of a political mastermind.

Ted slid closer to her. If that were possible. He reached his right arm around her waist. She nestled into his embrace.

A meaningful moment passed between them. Now there were no more words. The rest of the crowd receded. It was just the two of them alone on a lifeboat in the middle of the Chesapeake

Bay.

But what could they do, there in front of everyone?

Ted felt he should say something, but what? A few more moments passed.

"You know…" Roberta said, suddenly shy, looking around. "Seafood is an aphrodisiac," she said, trailing her painted fingernail along the edge of the shell of the one remaining oyster.

"That so?" Ted said.

"Mmm-hmm."

Then, quickly hoisting the shell, Roberta slurped the boogery sea-meat into her mouth. Ted laughed. She smiled and swished it around. Ted stared at her, impressed. Then Roberta lunged for Ted's face. Their lips met in a slobbery kiss. Barely aware of what was happening, and drunk enough not to care what anyone else in the room said, Ted opened his mouth for some hot tongue action.

But instead of Roberta's tongue twining his, she passed the hot oyster right into Ted's mouth, wet and sloppy. Shocked, he swallowed. Down his gullet it went.

"Wow," Ted said, the oyster nestling into his gut. "Um, thank you?"

Roberta smiled, her eyes drowsy with sluttiness. She slid her palm along the top of his thigh under the table, only inches away from his member of Congress.

"So you're leaving us?" Roberta said.

"Well, now I don't know. What other charms you got up your sleeve?" Ted replied.

"Your Washington Monument."

"Um."

"Up my Washington Wizards Sleeve."

"Say what?" Ted said.

Surely this repartee was leading somewhere. But during the middle of all this, Ted was cognizant of a shadow at the edge of his vision. He turned and saw two large suits standing at his elbow next to the table: double-breasted, double-chinned blobs.

Ted turned his head slowly, comically away from the ministrations of Roberta to regard the men inside the suits. Indeed, they were round and corpulent. Each held a wide snifter of expensive Scotch. "Why, helloooooo…" Ted said in a Mrs. Doubtfire trill.

"Mr. Cruz, *hello*," one of the stuffed suits said. "Tucker McCann-Blandstein. And this is, as you know, Allagash Greenwood, Jr."

They pumped hands. "Boys. What can I do ya for?" Ted said, obviously distracted, looking through them. Did he recognize them?

"Senior staff?" Allagash queried.

"Okay."

"GOP?"

"Okay."

Greenwood, Jr. and McCann-Blandstein

"You don't remember us? Strategy meetings? Grand Old Party? This very back room here at Fizzywhigs?"

"Look boys, if you're asking do I remember you or do I not remember you, the answer is a resounding... *maybe*. By the way, have you met my Chief of Staff, Bob—I mean—Roberta Cratchit?"

Two meaty paws reached over the table to shake Roberta's hand, barely comprehending her presence, as the two men had long ago foregone their libidos for luxurious whiskeys and political influence, which was a shame, because Roberta was a stone fox.

"Mr. Cruz, I just wanted to tell you that your 'non-filibuster' filibuster was a thing of genius." This was Allagash talking.

"Yeah, I know it was," Ted drawled. "I did it."

"And what's the point of science if it hurts business, right? Hurts innovation?" said the other meat pile, McCann-Blandstein. "Obamacare is a nightmare and is one step away from the Gulag Archipelago."

"That is a given."

Allagash cut in: "And global warming. What's

that about? The science isn't settled. It's just not settled," he said, punctuating his words with his fat fingers and whiskey glass.

"Look guys. These are all great points you're making. But I'm having a private meeting with my staff here. Is there anything generally I can do ya for, or should you skeedat while the skedaddlin's groovy gravy?"

The two men looked at one another.

"Sir, with all due respect, we think you should run for the Oval Office. The country needs you. Real Americans need you. Let's take America *back*."

Ted couldn't contain himself. "Bah!" he yelled, wide-eyed. A blackness filled his insides like a hickory smoke. "Run for president, huh?"

"Yes. *Yes*, sir."

Ted leaned back, a complicated joy jiggling the many handsome locations of his face. "Are there any Republicans in office right now?"

"Sure, yes…"

"And don't Republicans hold the House and the Senate?"

"Yeah, but not the—"

"Presidency? Wasn't a Republican president before Obama? And wasn't Obama the worst president since Hubert Humphrey? Is it not a one inch putt for *any Re*pub at this point?"

"But—"

"Oh I'm sorry, is there a shortage of politicians in Washington, DC? And are the American people still voting for whoever raises the most money?"

"Sorry, I'm not following," the one named Tucker McCann-Blandstein said, the fat around his eyes crinkling like the butthole-like lines at the pinch-point where linked sausages touch.

"Ugh. I'll put it in lame-ass layman's terms so you and your boyfriend can understand. I. Am. Not. Seeking. Re. Election. Mother! Fucker!"

"But…"

"Now GTFO my face 'fore I get a thirst for the cholesterol-filled blood of plutocrats!" Ted raised his arm as if to strike at them and the two suits escaped back into the crowd.

Roberta laughed next to him. "Oh, Ted. Don't be such a Tedbeneezer Scruz!"

This didn't register though. Ted suddenly felt queasy with the altercation.

His stomach gurgled. An unpleasant constriction announced itself in his innards. Was it the oyster?

He involuntarily stood halfway. Things weren't looking good. The sea-booger was unhappy in his new home in Ted's belly, as the poors were in federal housing.

"I think I need to go to the mens," he said, suddenly afraid he would spill his insides all over the levitating table.

"Oh, mmm, Good idea," Roberta said, and exhaled luscious hot air into his ear, which only seemed to fan the flames of nausea poisoning his bloodstream. "Why don't I meet you there?"

"Ungh—"

"I'll be in in five minutes, puddin' pop. I'll knock on the door three times like this." And she knocked on the front of his pants ever so

Fig. 13.—Oysters.

slightly with the head of her middle finger.

"No, it's an—" He almost said emergency. It most certainly was rapidly becoming one. Waterfalls of pain wetted Ted's stomach. His mouth watered hotly.

Something nasty was coming up.

He sprung from the table. Ted's vision going warbled and sick, he Hussein-Bolted through the crowd to the bathroom... And to destiny.

CHAPTER TWO
Fat Magic

Ted burst through the mahogany door to the bathroom, terror in his veins like Robespierre. There were three stalls, all occupied.

He ran to the first one. "Oh God, oh God, please!" he shouted and banged on the door. He tried the next two. All were locked. Grumbles answered him. Coughs. And toilet paper rolls rolling.

Ted felt the vomit tickling at his tongue. Any second now his internal organs would explode out his nostrils. "Please, somebody, I need to get in there!"

"Not feeling so hot, Teddy Boy?" came a voice next to him.

Beleaguered, Ted spun and with ratcheting horror saw who it was. Ted jumped up in his skin. Like those of a zombie wombat, two beady eyes behind unstylish spectacles stared at him in the dusky light of the john.

"Karl Rove?"

"Raphael Edward 'Ted' Cruz?"

"What the hell are *you* doing here? I didn't invite you to my party. Aren't you dead? Politically, I mean?"

With ratcheting horror Ted saw who it was.

"Right you are, Teddy Boy. It's true. I *am* here. Not as a guest, though," Karl said and handed him a steaming, hot towel. "I'm working."

"Working? Working the room for contacts, you old snake in the ass?" Ted said, bile filling his mouth as he spoke and regarding the man before him: a puffed, puffy, nerdly, needly, bespectacled newt. It really was Karl Rove. Turd Blossom himself. T.B. Rove.

"I'm the bathroom attendant in case you hadn't noticed, shit stain." Karl said and proffered a small wicker basket of scented soaps.

Potpourri, jasmine and eucalyptus assaulted Ted's nostrils. His stomach listed to the side like the Lusitania and perspiration bubbled up all over his body. "It's the only job I could find in D.C. after my Romney meltdown in 2012 on Fox. And just in case you don't want to wind up like me, you'll run for president."

"Bah! Not you too!"

"I'm dead as a doornail in this town, Teddy Boy. Learn from my mistakes. Grab power by the short and curlies while you still have agency—while America is still hard for your hole."

"Am I hallucinating? Is it the oysters or are

you… not wearing pants?"

"We were partners, Ted. Don't forget that. You remember how we pulled the rug out from underneath Gore in '00? Even though more people voted for him, we used the gerrymandered-ass Erectoral College to our benefit? The stuff of genius—"

"Erectoral College?"

"—but somewhere along the line we lost something. The public sector? People think it's this huge windfall. Leave office and make a bunch of shitty, forgettable speeches to rich knobjobs for $200k or let's all go out to the lobby and lobby the House for some inverted conglomerate. It's supposed to be a capitalist's Disneyland here, but the cash just ain't there, Mack. *Especially* if you've got nothing to say. All us wonks are a dime a dozen, dude."

"Yeah, but. The no pants thing?"

Ted watched Karl slowly and methodically look down his torso at himself. It was true. Not a stitch below the maroon blazer with the logo of Fizzywhigs—a picture of a fizzy wig, on it. There was nothing there. Nothing except Karl's little chief of staff. Karl looked back up at Ted. "Can't afford 'em," said Karl plaintively, raising his shoulders. *"That's* why you need to become president. I'm here as an allegory. *Learn* from me. (Then maybe hook me up with some work!)"

"No. I'm going to vomit up this oyster, then I'm going to bone Roberta, then I am going to K Street."

Karl's face darkened. "Well, fine by me. But if you refuse to learn from a pantsless bathroom attendant like me, you will be visited this night by three other bathroom attendants. One immediately after you've thrown up your seafood platter, two immediately after, at the stroke of... oh, I don't know... whenever it floats their boats to teach you a lesson and some freaking manners."

"Bathroom attendants?"

"Run along to your toilet now, Teddy Boy."

"But they're all taken," Ted groaned and pulled at his collar. Hot. His neck was too hot.

Then Karl waved his hand and the door to the stall on the left flew open on its own. It was empty.

"What the hell?" Ted stood amazed. Only a second before there were legs under there, the sounds of men passing and gassing. But a wave of nausea washed away his curiosity, puke frothing behind his teeth.

He made for toilet.

But Karl grabbed his arm. "Before you go, can I interest you in a moist towelette?" he said, and stuffed it in Ted's hand.

"Fine! Whatever! God dammit!" Ted screamed and flew to the open stall.

Just in time. The door slammed behind him. Ted fell to his knees. With utmost anguish his innards flipped inside out: Ted puked everything he had into the toilet—even things he didn't know he'd eaten—through his esophagus, out into the air and finally splashing in the water. He looked down and saw floating there one little booger of the ocean, a dollop of oyster like a tiny brain on the surface of *la toilette*. An aphrodisiac, she'd said. Ted smiled.

He stood and wobbled in place. The demon expunged, Ted was feeling a might better. "Wow," he said and realized there was still upchuck on his lips. He took Karl Rove's towelette and wiped his face clean. Then he threw the towelette in the toilet and flushed it.

In the water the towelette seemed to grow in size, like a sponge. He stood and watched it spin, mesmerized that something so small could suddenly grow so big. *Something to do with Rove's fat*

"Can I interest you in a moist towelette?"

magic, he thought…

Then with a pang of joy he remembered that Roberta was going to barge in any second. In the interim, though, his johnson had softened, like President Johnson on the poor. Quickly, Ted unzipped his pants and, like Sisqó, unleashed the dragon.

He had to be ready.

"Hey, if you're gonna jerk the chicken, why don't you just stuff it in here, big fella?" a voice suddenly said.

Ted screamed. It was such a strange voice, and came from somewhere unexpected—down the middle of the stall wall. "What the—"

"Yeah, down *here*. In the Ol' Glory Hole," the voice said.

Ted fumbled with his Richard Milhous "Tricky Dick" Nixon, nearly stinging it in his zipper, desperate to hide himself. "Excuse me, but who the hell are you?"

"I'm the Bathroom Attendant of Constitutionality Past," the voice said through the glory hole. There was also the sound of tiny fifes and drums.

"Bullshit. You're that Idaho Senator dude from the airport bathroom or whatever. First dumbass Karl Rove, now *you*. No way. No *damn* way at *my* party this is happening! Security! Security!"

Ted went for the door. It wouldn't open—was locked.

"What?" He really yanked at it now, both hands. Still the door would not budge. "What the fuck!" Ted screamed. He was trapped inside.

"Help! Karl! Dammit! Hello?"

But no one answered.

Except the small, strange voice. "Sorry, Ted, but through *here* is the only way out," it said.

"How can this be? Was Karl Rove telling the truth?"

But before Ted could do or say anything else, the Ol' Glory Hole began to glow, Ted's pants magically unzipped, his dong flung out, pulled itself like it was trapped in a gravity beam to the Ol' Glory Hole, and to the sounds of teeny-tiny fife and drum (John Phillips Sousa meets Spike Jones) and a radiant blast of magical light, Ted's thang and his entire body was sucked through to the other side.

CHAPTER THREE
Snowbird

Eyes wide, breathing fast, barn door open, Ted rematerialized with a shout. "Gah!"

He was standing in another bathroom stall, the next one over. He could hear the toilet still running. Apparently Rove's towelette had clogged the thing. Water began to run across the floor, wetting his expensive shoes. Why couldn't Rove have used his rag for underpants instead?

There was a draft. Ted reached down and was about to sheathe his scepter when a voice interrupted him.

"No. Leave it out."

Ted jumped with fright.

He hadn't seen the turkey.

Standing down in front of him in the stall was a turkey—big-breasted, brown, a glorious, mottled fantail posterior and a radiant, red gullet like that of an old man's balls after a lengthy sauna session.

"Um… what?" Ted stuttered. "D-d-did you say someth—"

"I *said* 'Leave it out,' dude," the turkey said. "Turkey likey."

It was then that Ted saw the turkey was wearing a maroon blazer—and no pants, if that's weird for a bird—with the Fizzywhigs logo on it, same as Rove's.

"So it's true. What Rove said. Are you really the ghost of Christmas Past?"

"You idiot! Is it Christmas Eve?"

"No…"

"Damn straight. I said I'm the Bathroom Attendant of Constitutionality Past and that's what I am."

"H-h-how did you come by this profession?"

"Simple. I'm the bird they took the feather from for the quill pen they used to sign the Declaration of Independence. A fine flapping Philly pheasant I was. And as I'm sure you're well aware, Ben Franklin wanted the turkey to be the national bird instead of the boring-ass and bland-ass bald eagle no one likes."

"Wow. Well, I suppose it's an honor then. Wow," Ted said. His stomach was a war of but-

Wild Turkey.

"Turkey likey."

terflies again. Maybe his queasiness was coming back.

"You're damn straight. Now, come on, take my wing. I want to show you a few things."

"Take me where?" Ted said, afraid now. "We're trapped in here. Y-y-you're not going to suck me through that hole again are you?"

"Only if you buy me a drink first," said the turkey and grabbed Ted's hand. "Let's go!"

The turkey flung the stall door open. Ted was amazed to see not the bathroom at Fizzywhigs at all but open air. Dark sky, starlight. He peered out the door and saw the night sky over Washington, D.C.

A cool breeze tussled his locks. Upstairs and downstairs. The avian Attendant yanked Ted's arm and the two floated out over the city.

Cool air massaged them as they swirled through the skies, going commando like Air Force Rangers, dangling above the monuments and Mall.

They were really flying!

Ted and the turkey climbed and spun, dived and rolled. "Whoopee!" Ted giggled. "But I thought turkeys couldn't fly?"

"Hey, suck my dick, turkey jerky. Check this shit out!"

Presently the flying pheasant pulled them towards a bank of clouds. They whirled into the whiteness, like a cool, refreshing steam. Washington evaporated from view below.

A few titillating moments later they touched down onto land. It was still night. They were on a field. A few houses slept in the dark nearby. In the distance, black machines pumped the land— oil derricks.

"I recognize this place," Ted whispered.

"Yeah ya do," the turkey said and led them to

one of the slumbering houses. Before Ted could say anything they walked through the wall.

Inside, Ted understood. It was his childhood home. His father was an exec for a Canadian oil conglomerate and this was the house the company rented to his family outside of Calgary.

"Check this shit out!"

The house was quiet and still. Then his mother, forty years younger, tiptoed by. It was heartbreaking to be back, to see her and the old house. "Hi, mom," Ted said.

"Are you an asshole or do you not know how this works? Nobody can hear you."

"I was *just* saying *Hi,*" Ted whispered.

33

They followed his mother, wearing a white and red nightgown, down the hall. She stopped at a doorway and put her ear to it. She listened quietly. A faint, yet repetitive, shushing noise reached the hallway. The turkey pulled them through the door (and broke on through) to the other side.

"My old bedroom," Ted said with a smile. "Oh… Oh my God. *Ew*."

On the bed was a dark form, bathed in moonlight. It was a blanket—someone under it. The blanket went up and down in a repetitive motion that should have been obvious to anyone.

Just as Ted and the turkey saw what was happening, Ted's mother burst through the door.

"Raphael, what are you doing? At it again? No! No! Stop it! Stop it!"

The blanket flew off the bed. Evidently, young Ted had a flashlight under the blanket with him to aid him in his endeavors. "Mom! Get out of here!" young Ted whined.

"Raphael," his mother yelled. "If your father only knew, eh. You know we're Canucks!"

"Why!?" young Ted whined.

"What do you mean, *why?* You were born here!"

"I wish Canada never existed, eh," whimpered

the boy, trying to cover up what was in his hands.

"Give me that!" his mother shouted. There were a few moments of tussling. Finally, his mother was able to wrangle away what young Ted was holding—a large sheet of paper.

"This should be good," said turkey.

"Return it, eh!" young Ted cried.

Ted's mother stood back and unfurled the paper in the moonlight. She recited: "We the people of the United States, in order to form a more perfect union…"

"Mom!"

"The United State Constitution again, eh? What have you against Canada?"

"I hate Canada! I hate it, hate it, hate it!"

"Well aren't you a bag of milk!" his mother yelled, reaching for a scroll on a shelf. She unfurled it with ceremony and began to read: "Whereas the provinces of Canada, Nova Scotia, and New Brunswick have expressed their desire to be federally united into One Dominion under the crown of the United Kingdom of Great Britain and Ireland…"

"No!" young Ted screamed. "I despise of the Constitution Act, 1867! I despise of it!"

"Snowbird, eh! Shush it and listen!"

"No! I won't! Why do you hate freedom and pure, unregulated markets, mother, eh!?" Young Ted said and leapt through the window like an acrobat and took off across the Canadian tundra, wailing into the night.

Young Raphael runs away to America.

Older, ethereal Ted touched a finger to his cheek. A tear caught the moonlight. "It was the first time I ran away to America," Ted said. "But not the last—*Hey*, what the hell!?"

The turkey was behind his young mother, feathering his ghostly turkey wings over her body like French ticklers. He was grinding his turkey hips on her and gobbling seductively. "What's up

Mrs. C? Turkey's feelin' perky."

"Stop that!" Ted yelled.

"Why?"

"Stop it, eh, snowbird, eh! Eh! Eh!" Ted screamed.

"Alright, alright. Jeesh. Seen enough, then?" asked the twerking turkey.

Ted sniffled. "Yes."

The bird whisked them through the wall. Ted was expecting the plains of oil-rich Alberta again—he got something else...

Oil derricks on the Canadian tundra.

CHAPTER FOUR
Prognosticating

'Twas the night after a settlement, when all through the houses, all the lawyers were partying, even the spouses; the stock options were hung over the heads of associates with care, in the hopes that rich dividends would soon be there; the partners of Cooper, Carvin & Rosenthal were happy with their bread, meanwhile the tequila flowed like wine, and everyone was off their heads...

It was a party to be remembered in Texas for years to come. Legendary. But there sat one man alone, leaning on a Xerox, apart from the rest. Twenty-seven year-old Teddy Cruz, newly hired apprentice, sheepishly eyed the festivities as a sheep eyes a pack of wolves. Screams shook the room. A beer bottle broke on the wall over his head.

This was the scene older Ted and the Bathroom Attendant of Constitutionality Past stepped through the wall to witness… Both were speechless at the debauchery. "I mean, everyone needs to let off some steam every once in a while, but this is the turkey's bananas," the turkey said. Someone fired a six-shooter through the ceiling.

Legendary.

A door opened near where Teddy the Wallflower sulked. One of the partners stuck his head out and beckoned him inside. Young Ted went, and older Ted and the turkey followed on misty toes.

"Ted, I'd like you to meet someone. Kenneth Starr," said the partner. "Ken, this is one of our bright young bucks, Ted Cruz."

The two princes shook hands.

An hour later, the stern men stood around a table, glowing with importance. Their course was clear: Impeach President Clinton come hell or white water. Ted had wowed all and sundry with his immediate insightful insights. "What about the word 'is' here in Clinton's deposition, *There's nothing going on between us.*' Willfully obscure?" Hearing this, Kenneth leaned back smiling a grin so wide, and so lost in thoughts of imminent victory, that he fell backwards out of his seat. "By gum! We'll finally get that smarmy bastard out! I don't care if we have to spend $70 million of the taxpayers' money—that's right, $70,000,000 USD that we shouldn't have collected in the first place because the IRS is a corrupt fraud—to do it!" he prognosticated from the floor.

Later, Young Ted walked over to a blue dress hanging on the wall. "How did you get such a piece of *choice* evidence?" He gave it a sniff.

"How did we get it? How did Woodward and

Bernstein get the Watergate tapes?"

"An illegal informant stole classified FBI secrets and passed them to the liberal media. Um, did you *steal* this?"

"What? No. I meant we made it up on the spot. That dress's just a mockup we're using as a visual. Like an inspiration board."

"Oh. Ew, so this stain here is…"

"Yup," Starr said, grinning, and fell over in his chair.

Older Ted and the turkey watched with admiration as Ted and Ken sat down immediately to work on the impeachment. While the party of law raged outside, inside these two men worked for the betterment of their fellow man.

Later, in the wee hours, Kenneth addressed Ted: "Have you ever thought of public office, Ted? I mean, you have the bearing. You're an Adonis, the body, the pectorals, the abs, the toned, unique physique. It's what any office in this land requires. You've got it in spades, if I may call a spade a spade. This impeachment is going to make us famous. You should capitalize on it."

"Wow. No. I mean, sure. Yeah, but. I mean, wow. Sure, yeah, no, I don't know, I mean, wow, no, yeah, public—, I mean, wow. Wow…"

"The stuff of legend," said the turkey.

"I thought they couldn't hear us?" said Ted.

"You son of a—I was talking to you."

But this moment of hardness did not last. Both Ted and the Bathroom Attendant turkey watched with glowing pride as the two lawyers tucked back into their work.

Young Ted Cruz meets Ken Starr.

"Ah, the public sector," Older Ted said. "Wasn't long before I was W's domestic policy advisor, Solicitor General, the Senate," Ted said with a smile. He thought for a few moments. A winsome, wistful, winning look played on his face. "Jeez, I wish…"

"Yeah?" replied Turkey.

"Oh, nothing. It's just that I was having a conversation with two gentlemen of the GOP a while ago I'd like to have over—*Hey,* what the hell!?"

"You know, Kenny," the ghostly turkey said, standing behind Kenneth Starr and whispering in his ear. "I'm mostly dark meat. Well, at least where it counts, anyway."

"Get away from him! I thought they couldn't hear us?"

"Oh, gobble-gobbledygook!"

The turkey rolled his turkey eyes. "Boy, you're no fun for a first time ghost, I tell you." The tur-

"So what did we learn?"

key flapped his wings and whisked them back into an ethereal cloud. From inside the cloud, Ted heard the turkey's voice. "Well, that about wraps it up on my end. So what did we learn?"

Ted thought a moment. "Well—"

"Psyche! I don't give a shit. Okay, here we are."

CHAPTER FIVE
Chubb Rock

The first sound was rushing water.

In the brief few, eternal moments before Ted's eyes materialized with the rest of his body, in the blackness of time-out-of-mind, there was the sound of water—chiming clear and mystical; flowing—life-giver of the universe.

Then his body exploded back to reality in the bathroom stall at Fizzywhigs and it was a damned mess—a damned hot mess, I tell you. The toilet was still running, choked with Karl Rove's magic towelette. Ted stood in water up to his knees. Was the entire bathroom flooded? All of Fizzywhigs?

"Help! Help!" Ted banged on the door.

He spun around, dove at the toilet. Up to his shoulder in water, he plunged his hand down the pipe. Stretching as far as he could, his fingers just tickled the edge of something soft, the edge of the cloth of the towelette.

"Laying pipe, Ed?" came another bodiless voice.

Ted jumped up from the water. He knew where to look. "Help! Get me out of here!" he yelled into the hole in the wall. "Help!" He squinted through it, saw feathers. A giant, yellow beak. Heard tiny, booming canon. "I can't swim!"

"You know the drill, Ed," said the voice. This voice was deeper and raspier than the turkey's.

Ted didn't hesitate. He dropped trou and aimed his Chubb Rock at the Ol' Glory Hole. In a whooshing of color and light he was sucked into the next stall.

Pow!

Ted opened his eyes. Rising before him in the stall stood a massive bald eagle, ten feet tall, wearing a maroon blazer, resplendent with weapons: missiles, machine guns, canon, muskets, grenades, F-16's, B-22's, petards, bayonets, armored personnel carriers, carrier pigeons, Sherman tanks, MQ-9 Reapers and the like. Regal, the bird beamed power and might. And, strangely, he was eating another bird. Feathers floated down from the eagle's sharp, yellow beak and when the massive bird opened its mouth, Ted saw more maroon fabric.

The Bathroom Attendant of Constitutionality Present

"Are you the ghost of Christmas—I mean!—the Bathroom Attendant of Constitutionality Present? Wait, sorry. But is that the Ghost of—you know, the turkey from before? You're, um, eating?"

"And so the present dispatches the past," boomed the eagle. "The only reality is *now*."

Ted gulped.

The eagle finished swallowing the turkey and knocked open the door. Cool air filled the stall. Ted breathed in, saw the same delicious, federally-funded view as before expanding outward. The eagle enfolded Ted in its huge wing and they launched into the night like a Cruz missile.

As before, a sleeping Washington D.C. rolled out beneath them. Snug in the eagle's down like America's weaker NATO allies snug in her military supremacy, Ted noted each building and monument, fun factoids for each peppering his noodle as they passed overhead.

But the bird did not linger in the skies. It was a hands-on bird. A claws-on bird. That is to say, the eagle laid waste to all they saw with its Yankee fecal waste…

They swooped down over the streets of Georgetown. Air buffeted them as they glided between trees, the quaint streets lined with colonial brick houses. In an enclave of small clapboard homes behind a converted horse stable forgotten by the D.C. elite, save the noble working classes—assistants, pages and interns—the proud American eagle landed on the cobblestones in a great flapping of wind like an Apache Helicopter, Ted Cruz his copilot.

"Eagle bird, do I know this place?" Ted whispered into the feathers.

"This place knows you," replied the eagle.

They went to one home in particular and passed through the wall. The home was small, modest. They went into the bathroom. "Hey, what the hell! Wow! Roberta!"

It was Ted's sexy assistant, Roberta. She lounged in a tub filled with bubbles. Gentle music played, soft light and water accentuating the curves of her breasts that hung as heavy and succulent as melons on the vine from her chest. She lifted a shapely leg from the suds and water trailed down her calf and thighs. Her eyes were half closed, murmured to herself while trailing her hands down her stomach, "Ooh, Ted…"

The eagle screeched. "Wrawk! Whoops, we'll come back to this!"

They dove downward through the floor into the living room. Roberta was there—fully pant-suited—with a small boy. They were in the middle of some heated debate. They sat in front of a computer.

"Timmy, you *have* to," Roberta said.

"I don't want a government handout!" the boy wailed. "I want the freedom of choice!"

"But Timmy, listen. You have a pre-existing condition. Your asthma. This is important. Also, we *have* to sign up or we'll be fined."

Surviving healthcare.gov.

"An individual mandate is a species of tyranny. It's a negative externality masked as a positive one. I don't want a handout if it means increased premiums for other honest Americans. Their tax burdens are already too heavy… and wasteful. That healthcare.gov is called a 'marketplace' smacks of the bitterest irony."

Roberta stared at her son. She was silent. There was obvious pride on her face that she was trying to hide.

"Her boy is a testament to the virtues of America," boomed the eagle. "A true patriot squeezed from her womb."

The true nature of the externality.

"I didn't even know Roberta had a kid. Jeez, some boss I am," Ted said.

"An honest oversight, Senator. You were busy running the world from the Legislative Branch. But that will soon be all over, won't it? Does the GOP not control the House and the Senate? Is the presidency not won by that who raises the most money?"

"Oh." Ted wavered. A look of worry came over his face. His eyebrows did the worm. He rubbed his six-pack absentmindedly. "Well, now I don't know. I don't know about all that. Wow. Young Timmy here sure reminds me of me when I was a youngin', when I was just a young Canadian lad."

"'Tis true."

"What will happen to him?" Ted asked the mighty, armed bird. "Will the Cratchits be forced to give in to tyranny—*Hey*, what the hell are you doing!?"

The eagle had floated over Roberta and Timmy. He flapped his wings and turned, his regal eagle rump over their heads.

"Only time will tell," said the bird and rained down a mail sack's worth of invisible bird shit onto them. Unbeknownst to Roberta and Timmy, eagle feces sparkled transparent in the ethereal plane on their heads and shoulders.

"I'm feeling good tonight, Timmy. I'm feeling suddenly blessed. Blessed with the American spirit. Tell you what. Let's not do this," Roberta said, and shut down her computer.

"God bless us, every one!" sang Little Timmy.

And they hugged.

"Wow," Ted said, "This was—"

In an instant Ted and the eagle were flying again.

It seemed that the Cratchit's home was only the first stop on a full night's journey…

All across the city, good Americans did their best to lead honest, productive lives. But it was not easy. Sin, laziness and government handouts were as abundant as thieves in the night. The eagle fixed that. The eagle fixed it with its invisible, indivisible spirit. The eagle shat on them. The eagle shat on them *all*.

A CEO sat at a desk, his pen wavering over a stack of papers. It wasn't until a Fat Man of the eagle's guano burst atop his hairpiece that courage found him. He signed the papers… Their one remaining factory on American soil would move to Bangladesh, ensuring life, liberty and the pur-

suit of happiness for his shareholders. And outside that factory, the eagle unloaded on the pro-
testing union workers. "They want those jobs so
bad, they know where to find them," said gruffly
the symbol of economic freedom. The agitators

The eagle shat on them all.

dispersed to their homes to reflect on the entre-
preneurial spirit. A soon-to-be previously gay
man walked into a sexual re-orienting facility for
treatment. His sin would drop away like the crust

of a (homosexual) chrysalis. Soon he would marry a beautiful woman and raise two point five beautiful children, thanks to the "giving" spirit of the eagle. An economically disadvantaged student worked his way through college. A father downloaded the instructions for building an AR-15 with a 3D printer. A little guy got the loan he needed to start his business. This little guy was going to take Amazon and Walmart to task in the open market. His store was going to be called Walmazon. And the banker who risked everything to give that little guy the loan? Why, he profited as well. Then the eagle flew out into the heartland. America. They swooped over the scrublands of Arizona, New Mexico and Texas, where exhausted volunteers protected American shores from illegals and ISIS invaders. The great bird dropped a megaton of ethereal droppings on them, giving them strength for one more sortie, one more walk along the watchtower walls. They swooped over a Civil War reenactment, the Stars & Stripes and the Stars & Bars waving proudly, symbols of states rights, but also the might of the United States, but also, it must be noted, the freedom of states to decide what's best for them, because this is the United States, emphasis on the

States part. The eagle pinched out a dollop of its spirit poo, and so the battle of Appomattox was enjoined with renewed vigor, with possibly a different and more beneficent outcome this time. "Some gave all," intoned the bird. And the eagle turned his flight back east. In a heartbeat, it seemed to Ted, they were flying low once again over the streets of Washington D.C. In the West Wing, finally alone after a long

Archibald V. Quilms, Founder & CEO of Walmazon, Inc.

day of tyranny, President Obama unfurled his secret prayer mat, lay it on the floor facing east and knelt down on it, murmuring in a foreign tongue. Harry Reid polished off a bill that would stifle innovation. John Kerry lied about something. Hillary drew up the plans for the assault on Benghazi. The NSA read your email. The bird unloaded his butt-mud on them all. "Benjamin Franklin... What a bunch of horseshit," said the eagle. "Or should I say turkey shit? Okay, so the turkey is the national bird? Then what? What do we eat on Thanksgiving? Eagle? How stupid. How so *very* stupid. Franklin spent half his life in *France* and I think that tells us something. Well, *après moi, le déluge...*"

The eagle swooped low over Georgetown again.

"Back to Bob's?" Ted said hopefully into the down of the eagle.

"Mmm," purred the bird.

They came to the enclave once again and went through the wall. It was the same bathroom as before. Roberta lifted a gorgeous gam from the water. It looked like the Titanic tipping upward before it sank. Gorgeous.

"Oh, wow," Ted said.

Then Roberta raised her other leg and straddled the tub at the knees. She lifted herself up, her ass dripping water, and displaying her lovely femininity to Ted and the American Eagle. The vision of a lovely dark bush, like amber waves of grain, greeted their eye sockets. Before Ted could engage with the vision fully though, in a strange effect of time and space, the bird dove headlong into the center of Roberta's darkness and they disappeared.

A strange effect of time and space.

CHAPTER SIX

Yuppers

Ted cannonballed into the Fizzywhigs bathroom stall. The toilet water was at his chest now—and rising. Though his feet were on the floor, he struggled to stay afloat. He pumped his arms wildly.

"Rove!" Ted screamed. "Rove! Turd Blossom! Help!"

Drowning thoughts blotted out Ted's brain. Water, water everywhere—rushing, flooding, whooshing, pulling at his legs like an undertow of poors.

"Help! Help! Anybody! Swim—!" he

screamed. He spun around. He kicked at the door. He began to panic at the disco. "—I can't!"

Suddenly, an idea came to him. A desperate one... He held his breath, ducked his head under the water... Yes! There it was. Down in the water on the wall: another hole of glory.

"—I can't!"

Struggling mightily in the deluge, Ted reached for his trousers. Whatever erection he had ogling Roberta in her tub had dwindled with the fear of drowning; he could no more get a hard-on now any more than a Chinaman could get to heaven.

But a fully was not necessary... Affixing Tab A to Slot B, Ted felt the pinch of time-space and was vacuumed through to the next stall...

What fresh hell was this?

A mad frenzy of beaks, wings and sword-sharp feathers blinded him. Squawking, chirping and crunching deafened him. A flapping riot of birds knocked him back against the wall.

Covering his eyes he could just make out what was happening through his fingers.

A wake of vultures was tearing apart the eagle. There might have been a thousand of them, these voracious buzzards, if there were a dozen. The vultures used their long necks to pull the eagle's muscle tissue up from its body like long strands of spaghetti.

So this was the fate of American freedom, Ted thought. Each feeding bird representing one of America's nasty little enemies, banded together to destroy the great bird when it was at its weakest—in the john. Horror twisted Ted's soul. He wished to be back drowning in the first stall rather than witness this indignity. *Strange though,* Ted thought. *Not a maroon blazer on one of them.*

Which one was the Bathroom Attendant of Constitutionality Future though? He wanted to get on with it. Ted tapped the shoulder of the monster closest to him. "Are you the—um, are you? Excuse me, are you the—?"

Enemies of the State.

The birds stopped their nasty masticating with horrible speed.

All turned to him, leering with dead eyes, peering into Ted—sniffing out his weaknesses, divining his soft points of entry.

Ted pressed his back against the wall. The flock gobbled meanly at one another in brief conversation.

Then they came at him.

But before dinner plans could unfold, the stall door flung open.

The vultures all turned to look. There was a moment of silence, hesitation, fear. Something in the air frightened them. A scent. The vultures screamed and flapped away out the door.

He was alone.

Ted stood breathing fast, staring out the stall.

It wasn't the D.C. night sky again out there, but a vague grayness. A gray nothingness. Wisps of fog rolled into the stall from this nothing.

Ted stepped forward, saw that there was grass, wet and dingy, trailing away from the stall, and felt a desolate, heartless breeze.

Then through the dismal mists he saw a figure approaching. Silent, floating, it came across the grass.

It was coming for Ted.

And Ted was afraid.

He shouted into the formless fog, the figure of the future floating toward him. "I'm all better now! I'm fixed! Please don't show me anything more. I know what's coming!" he yelled and smooshed his Chief of Staff against the wall—to no avail, "Yes, yes, I die, and America dies with me! I know the drill. I do. Just send me back. I'll do it! I'll stick to the public sector! So really, it would be a waste of your time. I'm sure there are less repentant politicians out there in need of your services! Please!" Ted cried. He was at loose ends. He was crying—really crying.

The figure—the thing that had scared off the deadly birds—loomed nearer in a cloak of mist, death gray and vague and desolate.

Finally, the figure stepped from the fog.

It was a penguin.

A small thing, it stood no higher than Ted's knee. It was black-backed, had a white belly and orange ears, puffy as a throw pillow.

The penguin blinked at Ted, shuffled its feet back and forth on the moist grass. It blinked again.

"Are you—?"

Ted saw the penguin wore a maroon blazer.

"Yes—I see that you are," Ted said.

The penguin made a tittering little noise and reached out a tender wing to Ted. Ted stepped forward. He took the wing and the two tottered from the stall into the mist.

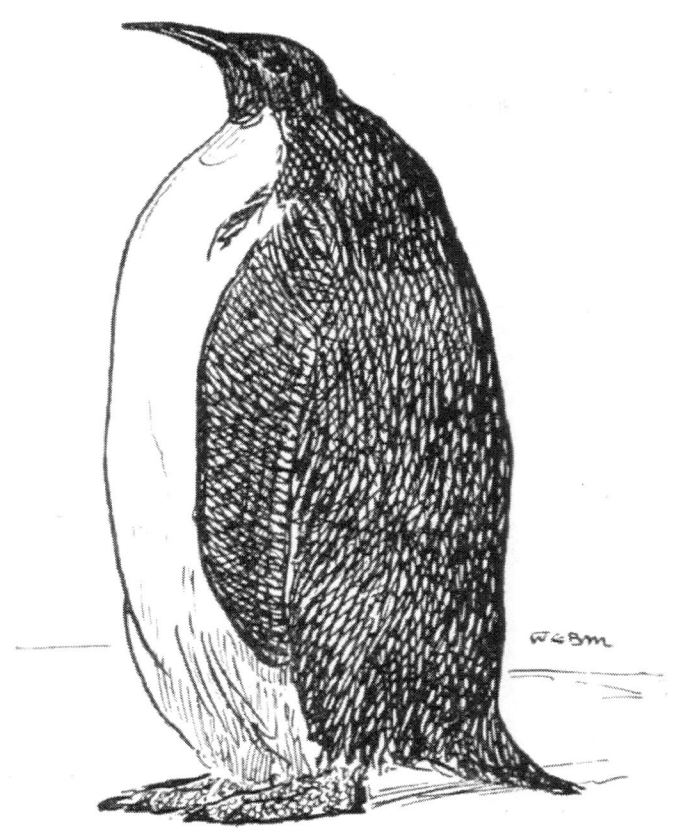

The Ghost of Constitutionality Yet to Be

It wasn't long before Ted realized where they were. Indeed, the Bathroom Magic had not sent him far.

They were on the D.C. Mall. All was droopy

and sad. Dejected cherry trees squatted bare and bloomless. Rising up into the gray, wet fog Ted saw the Washington Monument as they passed by it, dilapidated, missing masonry here and there, which, as a member of the illuminist Temple of Masons, surely caused the first president to roll over in his grave.

Voices came across the lawn. They walked toward them. As they got nearer the crowd, Ted felt his nerves pale.

"Really, this isn't necessary," he said down to his little friend, the silent harbinger. "Are you not going to talk? Am I to infer everything I see? Oh, spirit! Please! Say something!"

The penguin of Constitutionality Yet to Be only tottered forward. People—gray shapeless forms—wafted by.

"Is this the afterlife?"

The penguin did not answer, only walked forward in stony, ungainly silence, dark desolation permeating the air.

At last they came to the steps of the Capitol Building. The crowd of gray ghosts was thicker here. The penguin and Ted walked among them, went to the front. Was Ted buried here? Was this his funeral? It certainly had the feel of a funeral.

People stared with vacant eyes up at the steps. A sadness floated like a disease among the cloaked beings.

Ted thought to ask what was happening, from the penguin or from the wan creatures surrounding him. But he knew better. This whole thing was about sitting back like at an IMAX and letting the morals whale you with the money shot.

Suddenly, up at the top of the steps a great light was illuminated. A strange scene was unveiled. There was a throne. Flowers, soldiers. A dirge of fife and drum played from unseen speakers. Then a procession, of glowing and golden people in robes and jewels, split the crowd.

Ted stepped to one side to avoid being crushed under a bejeweled carriage finely decorated in filigree. The carriage then climbed the Capital Steps, and at the top a group emerged from it, royalty, handsomely appointed, dressed in the finest finery, gathered around the throne. A wizened old woman sat down in it, the evil palpable about her eyes, which cast themselves now on the assembled rabble below with regnant disdain.

Then some kind of religious figure made a sermon. The language of it was hard for Ted to follow. But what happened next was not. It was *very* digestible. The priest stepped behind the throne and placed a crown atop the woman's head. "Here ye! Here ye!" he shouted. "All hail Queen Chelsea the First!"

"Long live Queen Chelsea," droned the assembled crowd.

"Good Lord, is that Chelsea Clinton?" Ted asked the silent fowl, but he knew the answer: *Yuppers.*

"Bend your knees, slaves!" shouted the priest. "Bend them or die!" All around Ted the crowd fell to their knees with a mechanical unanimity. Ted looked closer and saw that they were all wearing knee contraptions, which forced them to the ground. Looking closer he saw there were words written on the knee contraptions. The words said: "Auto-Genuflectors Cour-

"Here ye! Here ye! All hail, Queen Chelsea the First!"

tesy of Obamacare—Allah Bless America."

Then a claxon blared the words: "Disperse now, go back to your happy lives, disperse now, go back to your happy lives…"

A word was spoken by Queen Chelsea, the First of Her Name, atop the steps and her guards began to fire their weapons into the crowd, sweet-ass laser guns.

A word was spoken by Queen Chelsea.

The tired, gray creatures still on their knees turned their shoulders to the assault. They began to crawl away. Some were vaporized by the weapons, straight up the butt, but some disappeared into the dismal atmosphere to attend to their happy lives. Ted saw with sadness that it did not seem to the people to matter which.

A cool laser explosion launched a divot from the grass near Ted's shoe and he and the penguin shuffled off.

The invisible duo waddled through Washington, sadder than any bleak winter moor. Eventually, they walked the streets of Georgetown and came to the cul-de-sac behind the horse stable. Roberta's house.

"Please, spirit penguin. I don't know if I'm ready for this."

Still rocking the silent treatment like a boss, the penguin waddled through the wall and Ted followed.

Inside was a shocking sight.

It was Tiny Timmy, all grown up. He was tethered to a treadmill, and running on it at the maximum speed. He was sweating, his body working hard, but his eyes were far away, dead to the world.

"But that's good right? He had asthma!" Ted exclaimed. Then he saw Timmy was wearing a mask attached to a huge machine. It breathed for him. And he was chained to the treadmill. Directly in front of him was a TV screen that said simply: "Obamacare is life, Obamacare says be healthy, Obama is the way…"

And Ted understood. Timmy had held out as long as he could, but eventually he had buckled under the predatory fees. He was forced to get healthcare for his asthma. Timmy was alive, but he was dead inside.

"But where's Roberta? Is she—? Is she—?" Ted couldn't say the words. He knew she was gone. The penguin did not answer and led him back outside and they went downtown again.

An hour or so later they came to K Street, lined with tumbledown huts. One of the huts had a handmade, vintage shabby-chic sign that read: "The Heritage Foundation."

"Am I buried here?" Ted asked of the penguin. Silently, the penguin walked through the wall. Ted followed.

An old woman sat on the dirt floor in front of a ball of glowing light. Ted saw it was Roberta! Much older, but still sexy as hell, he felt a twinge of pain as he realized she had followed him to the private sector. He watched her reach into the glowing light-wad and move her fingers about inside it. Ted looked into the light and saw the internet. This was the internet now.

"I do not approve of the coronation of Queen Chelsea the First," Ted saw Roberta had scribbled into the floating ball of light. She then moved her fingers to a cloudlet of mauve inside the light labeled "SEND." Thus Roberta posted the think-piece to her blogwwwlumen, the last free thoughts ever published in this land.

Roberta posts to the blogwwwlumen.

Within seconds, bells were going off in the NSA, which was not a building now, but a fine spray housed in subatomic nano-biomes joined to the very molecules of oxygen the world over. Al-

gorithms on the air sniffed out Old Roberta's re-
bellious tone. Seconds later, thugs in royal robes
and riot gear battered down the hut's door, filled
a blackout bag with Roberta's head, and dragged
her away into the fog.

"They Galileoed her," Ted lamented to the
penguin. "Spirit, my soul has broken with these
sights. Please… no more."

But still the penguin waddled on…

Hours of waddling later they came to a board-
ed-up building ensconced in cobwebs, riddled
with bullet holes. They went inside.

It was impossible to breathe here. Mold and
mildew and a seafood smell of supreme moistness
that reached to the levels of toxic waste assaulted
Ted's nostrils, made his head wobble and nearly
knocked him to his knees.

Ted regained his composure and took stock
of his environment. "Spirit penguin," he said, "I
believe I know this place. Strange, is it…?" The
penguin simply lifted his cute little wing towards
the back. "There? Am I to go there? What's
there?" he whimpered.

Ted slowly, very slowly, marched forward.
The building was dark, the wood on the walls was
very dark. The penguin followed silently. They

came to a door and went in. Then Ted knew the place.

"The back room of Fizzywhigs!" Ted shouted. "I knew it. Oh, but it has fallen on bad times, eh?"

The penguin did not answer, only pointed his wing again towards the back.

"The bathrooms?" Ted asked.

"Oh, but it has fallen on bad times, eh?"

A dip of the flightless bird's head seemed to be the only answer of agreement. More afraid than ever, Ted pushed at the bathroom door. It did not give easily. He put his shoulder into it and it opened.

The room was black—a gust of old, evil air raised the hair on his head. The penguin pushed at Ted's buttocks and they went in.

Using spirit magic, the penguin illuminated the bathroom and the scene of utmost horror it contained.

Ted screamed like a woman.

First things first, there were skeletons in disarray everywhere. The room was dry but had obviously been flooded decades before and not been cleaned or repaired. Mold crawled the walls. Did the people here drown? The skeletons wore the tatters of expensive suits. A maroon blazer wrapped a pantsless, shall we say 'big-boned' skeleton like a shawl in the corner.

The penguin pushed him towards the stalls.

"Hey!" Ted protested.

But the penguin still pushed, pushed him into the first stall. And then it kept pushing Ted.

"What are you doing? There's nowhere to

go!"

The penguin grew in size.

Or was Ted shrinking?

Both. Ted was shrinking and there was nowhere for him to go besides atop the toilet as the penguin shoved him.

Suddenly Ted was only three feet tall, then two, then only a few inches. "Help!" he screamed! "Help!"

Ted fell into the toilet. Water all around him. The bowl of the toilet was as big as a lake; he began to thrash in it. The penguin reached a wing for the handle.

"NOOOOooOOOoOOOOooooooO!!!!"

But it was too late. The penguin flushed and Ted dwindled down the toilet to drown forever in the murky depths of some wasteful municipal waste management facility.

"NOOOOooOOOoOOOOooooooO!!!!"

CHAPTER SEVEN
Flutter and Fade

But in the pulse of a heartbeat, in the snap of a synapse, Ted burst back to reality like a frozen pipe, his psychedelic visions evaporating away.

"NOOOOooOOOoOOOOooooO!!!!" Ted's voice crackled.

He was in the bathroom and he was wide awake. Ted sat on the floor, hugging the porcelain throne.

It had all been a dream!

"It was just a dream!" Ted shouted in the very real bathroom stall, sitting up. "Good gravy, it *must* have been that terrible oyster!"

Joy ran rampart over his heart.

There was still time!

Yes!

He would run.

Run he would for the presidency!

The turkey, the eagle, the penguin—the good birds of his better self had shown Ted the light. "Silly Rove, Ol' Turd Blossom… thank you!" shouted Ted, his hands clasped together.

"Good gravy!"

Suddenly, the path for him was very clear. He would run back out to the retirement party and call it off. Yes—not only would he *not* retire, but he would kick that shit into overdrive. To the whirr of smartphone video recorders he would then and there announce to the world his intentions. People would cheer. He'd grab those two fat GOP wonks by the lapels, knock the snifters out of their paws, and sign off on his candidacy. Oh, the joy! He would sweep Roberta up, kiss her on the lips, undo her pantsuit, make love to her on a pile of United States Constitutions, kiss her on the other lips. He'd give Little Timmy a referral to a really good doctor, one he could pay for out of pocket of his own free will. He'd give tax breaks to the needy: the CEO trailblazers who held the goodly shareholder's lives in his hands. Oh, he would be president... He would most certainly be president!

Ted stood up in the stall. He saw that his suit jacket had clogged the toilet. There was water all over the bathroom floor, but he was so happy with himself and what he was about to do, it did not register much. "So *that's* what caused the dreams! Wow!" he said and waded towards the door.

"First thing I'm gonna do, I'm gonna get me a website, tedcruz.com, and then I'm going to hook up an announcement venue. Gotta be somewhere... hip. Lotta youngin's around that will want to avoid being fined if they don't attend! Then I'm gonna..."

Ted flew from the bathroom door caterwauling like a Viking with a crab leg up his rectum, "Ayeeeeeaaahhhh!!!!!"

From the lavatory, Ted bursts forth to announce his candidacy... "Ayeeeeeaaahhhh!!!!!"

The main problem though—and it turned out to be a mighty big one—was that Ted hadn't realized exactly how much water had flooded the bathroom during the hour he was dreaming in there with the door locked…

A deluge of thousands of gallons of water exploded out with him and flooded the Fizzywhigs backroom like an act of God.

People screamed. The undertow took them down. Tables, chairs were swamped, people of high society and low trying to get away from the crashing water. There were the sounds of breaking glass, furniture rupturing. The bar fell over into the wall, and the giant mirror behind it unhinged itself, fell, and exploded on the floor with all the bottles of liquor. The water swept out of the back room and into the restaurant in the front. The sounds of surprise, screaming and crashing furniture there too reached the back room.

Ted fell and rolled in the surf. He was in danger of going under, of drowning. There was a table, floating. He reached for it. Grabbed hold of it. Pulled himself up onto it like a life raft.

Still, the water rose.

He observed the carnage. Everywhere people were screaming, going under, dying, losing their pearls. "Roberta! Roberta!" he yelled into the boiling ocean in the room. "Where are you!"

"Ted! Ted!" Ted heard.

He scanned the room (not for pussy, but for life). Yes! Over there, he saw Roberta fighting the deluge, arms flailing wildly in the water. He began to paddle the table over to her. Roberta went under, Ted reached out and grabbed her hand. He pulled her up onto the table.

"What the hell happened? Did you do this? This flood?"

"I-I d-d-don't know. The science isn't settled on that. Look, hurry! Where are those two wonks? Blandman and the Allegheny? I got an announcement I gotta make!"

"I think they drowned!"

"Oh!"

Still the water rose.

The table wobbled on the flood. Ted tightened his grip on it and Roberta tightened her grip on Ted. It wasn't long before their little lifeboat caught the tide in the backroom and they flowed out of the restaurant, the flood swamping cars and shrieking pedestrians on the streets all around

The rescue of Roberta.

them. Fizzywhigs was only a couple blocks from the Potomac River and within minutes the racing flood reached it, and Ted and Roberta flowed over the banks out onto the river, heading for the Chesapeake.

...Swamping cars and shrieking pedestrians.

They were soaked to the bone, their bodies steaming with heat and hot breath.

"What did you want to tell the wonky fatties?" asked Roberta after a time, watching the lights of Washington and Alexandria flutter and fade behind them as Ted's flood swamped the electrical grid.

"Oh, that I wanted to run for president."

"Ted!" Roberta screamed with delight and fell upon him.

He patted her on the head. "Doesn't seem to be a point to it now though, does it?"

"Hmm, maybe. You can be president of this here table though."

"Really?"

"Sure. In no time we'll be in the Chesapeake Bay," Roberta said, snuggling up close to Ted on the floating table. "There're a ton of oysters there. And those are aphrodisiacs."

"That so?" Ted said reaching around her and holding Roberta close.

They made love on the table and then the table sank slowly below the rising waves.

The End

ABOUT THE AUTHOR

Well, let me tell you about good ol' Lacey Noonan. Lacey lives on the east coast with her family. When not sailing, sampling fine whiskeys or making veggie tacos, she loves to read and write steamy, strange, silly, psychological and sexy stories. During daylight hours she is a web designer and developer, but mostly a mom.

For more information on Lacey Noonan, why not point your browser snake at:

Amazon Author Profile
amazon.com/author/laceynoonan

Mailing List
http://eepurl.com/bEeNgv

Facebook
facebook.com/laceynoonan123

Twitter
twitter.com/laceynoonan

Email
laceynoonan123@gmail.com

Other Books by *Lacey Noonan*

A Gronking to Remember:
Book One in the Rob Gronkowski
Erotica Series

Leigh has a serious problem. And it's driving a "spike" between her and her husband Dan. When she accidentally witnesses the NFL's biggest wrecking ball, Rob Gronkowski of the New England Patriots, do his patented "Gronk Spike," she is suddenly hornier than she's ever been. This causes her to go on a rampage of her own—a rampage of "self-discovery." And soon everyone's lives have changed. Romance! Sports!

A Gronking to Remember 2: Chad Goes Deep in the Neutral Zone (Book Two in the Rob Gronkowski Erotica Series)

The saga continues! When Leigh spurns his advances at a party he throws in her honor, Dan's friend Chad kidnaps her, stealing her away to his personal New England Patriots Shangri-La, a secret Man Cave hundreds of feet below sea level he affectionately calls his "Chadmiral's Quarters." There she learns about a side of Gronk she'd never known, changing her life forever. Secrets will be revealed—Gronktastic secrets. Possibly the greatest sequel ever written. Makes the original look like a certified *piece of shit!*

Seduced by the Dad Bod: Book One in the Chill Dad Summer Heat Series

Amanda's back from college for the summer, sexy and bored. Mr. Baldwin is a chill dad who loves swimming, singing '90s hits, Super Soakers and has a body like a big sack of wet sugar. What happens when these two star-crossed lovers cross paths? And oh yeah—he's her boyfriend's dad? Uh-oh! By turns devastatingly erotic and incisive, this first installment of Lacey Noonan's hot new summery Dad Bod saga will leave you questioning everything in your life.

Hot Boxed: How I Found Love on Amazon

Hot Boxed is the story of Randi, a 20-something girl working at an Amazon Distribution Center who wants more out of life. Assuming she'll work there forever, a name pops up on her scanner that ignites her passions. Does she have the courage to break the chains that bind her, to step out of her dreary life and do something so, so, so crazy to get what she wants? Find out in this super-steamy story!

I DON'T CARE IF MY BEST FRIEND'S MOM IS A SASQUATCH, SHE'S HOT AND I'M TAKING A SHOWER WITH HER ... BECAUSE IT'S THE NEW MILLENNIUM

Life for Jason is one wild experience after another. But then one night, a chance encounter dredges up a long-forgotten mystery, and suddenly he is trapped on a roller coaster of wildness. Is it more wildness than he can handle? Now he is on the run with his star-crossed lover. Will they reach a shower in time, or will the natural heat that burns within her consume them both? Literally, the steamiest book you will read all year!

I DON'T CARE IF MY SASQUATCH LOVER SAYS THE WORLD IS EXPLODING, SHE'S HOT BUT I PLAY BASS AND THERE'S NOTHING HOTTER RIGHT NOW THAN RAP-ROCK

Star-crossed lovers Jason and Starla are back in this devastatingly sexy and fun sequel. On the run from the devious Lemaire family and lost in the woods for weeks looking for the rendezvous that will get them to Starla's homeland, they are at their wits end when Jason abruptly joins the rap-rock band 311 (currently on tour with the Lilith Fair), throwing their whirlwind romance—and their very lives—into jeopardy. Welcome to the new millennium! Or is it?

THE BABYSITTER ONLY RINGS ONCE

This is NOT your typical babysitter story... One night when Sophie realizes she's left something scandalous at the Lindstrom's—the affluent family she has babysat for years now—she goes against all the fibers of her being and decides to get it back—no matter what, even if it means more scandal. Find out what Sophie recovers in this seriously HOT and suspenseful story by Lacey Noonan.

EAT FRESH:
FLO, JAN & WENDY AND THE FIVE DOLLAR FOOTLONG

"God damn, marketing events are bitch." And so begins the sexy, wild adventures of our three protagonists, Jan, Flo and Wendy—the three hottest stars of the contemporary TV commercial scene. After a fight with Wendy's agent, the girls take it upstairs to Flo's VIP hotel room, where they soon discover the pleasures of each other's bodies—as well as the very valuable, last remaining Five Dollar Footlong at the event. Caution: Hottt!

SHIPWRECKED ON THE ISLAND OF THE SHE-GODS: A SOUTH PACIFIC TRANS SEX ADVENTURE

Shipwrecked on the Island of the She-Gods is a seriously sexually-charged adventure of heart-pounding exotica that doesn't skimp on story or skimpily-clad native girls with "a little something extra." And it's a little something extra that Noah, Julian and Owen will experience over and over in the steamy jungle, along the shores and atop towering mountains until they're begging for mercy. And then begging for more

THE HOTNESS: FIVE BURNING HOT NOVELLAS

PREPARE TO BE TURNED THE HELL ON. Here are five novellas that will titillate and drive you wild, running the gamut of erotic fantasies. If you've ever wanted all of Lacey Noonan's books in one easy, accessible place for one low price, then this is the book for you, sexy-pants. Contains the novellas: *Submitting the Landlord; Hot Boxed: How I Found Love on Amazon; The Babysitter Only Rings Once; I Don't Care if My Best Friend's Mom is a Sasquatch, She's Hot and I'm Taking a Shower With Her (...Because It's the New Millennium);* and *Eat Fresh: Flo, Jan & Wendy and the Five Dollar Footlong.*

The Dishes Are Done, Man!

Made in the USA
San Bernardino, CA
20 December 2015